Karl Avery

Originally on the path to becoming a British sprinter, the author's varied career has included encounters with fascinating people, diverse places, and unique roles. Notably, during the Covid-19 pandemic, he served with the UK Emergency Services as an ambulance crew member. This experience inspired the development of the 'ribbon tree,' a symbol of hope for patients and their families. The tree, which he often passed, was bare of leaves but adorned with brightly colored ribbons tied to its branches.

Karl Avery

THE RIBBON TREE

AUSTIN MACAULEY PUBLISHERS®

LONDON • CAMBRIDGE • NEW YORK • SHARJAH

A CIP catalogue record for this title is available from the British Library.

ISBN 9781035872527 (Paperback)
ISBN 9781035872534 (ePub e-book)

www.austinmacauley.com

First Published 2024
Austin Macauley Publishers Ltd®
1 Canada Square
Canary Wharf
London
E14 5AA

This is a work of the heart, and I couldn't have done it without the support of my parents, Anne and Nigel, for believing I can achieve what I put my mind to and my son Lewis for thinking his dad is awesome all the time.

My special thanks are reserved for my inspiration and creative centre that comes from the love of my life. Thank you, Cassida, for always inspiring me to be creative and for your love of the characters and pushing me to let *The Ribbon Tree* grow from an idea to the page.

Prologue

War has broken out in Europe and the hopes of a nation rest with the bravery of the serving forces and volunteers that have chosen to make the ultimate sacrifice.

For some, this is a call to arms and the duty to serve is an honour and a duty to protect King and country, for others, this is a time of worry.

For a young man, it is a disaster. He has just proposed to the love of his life and is just waiting for the letter calling him to do his duty. His father served his country during the last war and made it back, he was never quite the same afterwards and he wonders how will this affect his future and that of his beloved.

Chapter 1
Jack's Story

"Mum, it's arrived." Jack calls out. "What do I do?" He adds.

"You need to speak to Martha," comes the reply.

It's 1942 and Jack, like other men his age, is being called to conflict, to protect his country and his family though his sense of duty is being called into question. He had planned to marry his fiancée Martha, having just proposed, then the war broke out. Having agreed to wait a while before walking down the aisle, this was certainly not what they thought would be happening. With the arrival of his conscript letter, Jack knows he has just two weeks before he reports to his training camp. Two weeks is not nearly enough time to organise himself, let alone, rush a wedding to the love of his life.

Martha was sitting, looking lovely as ever, by the stream where Jack had proposed on the outskirts of the village. As he got closer, he could see she was crying.

He sat beside her and as he put his arm around her, she looked up and asked, "What will we do?"

He looks at her with hope in his eyes and tells her everything will be alright. He hands Martha a note of how to write to him while he is away and he will write her as often as time allows. They embrace with reaffirming love before heading back to the village.

That night, Jack spoke to his parents about how they managed to survive during the last war being so far apart and with scarce communication. His mother, Eliza, tells him she always knew his father would be home, she felt it. His father, Thomas, was a different matter. He explained that the war changed him, he saw how barbaric people could be to one another for no good reason other than greed or power and he was a grocery store clerk before the war, so it all came as a shock to his system. Jack was aware that his father had come back a different man, he remembers his mother telling him about his temper before Jack's arrival. What Jack didn't expect was for his father to tell him that it was having Jack that saved him, when he got back from war he felt he had lost himself and the only part of him that returned was that which had learnt to survive in those dark places. Jack's mother was an angel, according to his father.

"She never gave up hope that I was there."

His mother had always spoken of their hardship in having a child and that Jack was their own little miracle. He was an only child, though his parents would have loved more, his arrival saw his father return to his old self and the horrors of war became a distant memory.

He embraces both parents, as his father heads to bed, his father reassures him with a warm embrace and his mother suggests some warm milk for Jack to ease him to sleep. Jack waits with his mother in the kitchen.

"You remember the stories I told you when you were a boy?" she says.

"Which one, Mother? There were so many." Jack replies.

9

As his mother passes him the warm milk, she tells him the story of a beautiful tree that bore not leaves or fruit yet shone majestically, covered with the most amazing array of 'ribbons'.

Jack interrupts.

He does remember the stories and that it was an old wives' tale of a wishing tree. When he asks his mother where she found it, she had no idea as she had been unable to find it again, she tells him she retraced her steps on many occasions after Jack was born and to no avail. Jack can't help but think, how is this helping, when his mother suggests that he spend some time before he has to report in, taking a walk in the woods to see whether he can find the tree.

"It's an old wives' tale, Mother, nothing more!" Jack exclaims.

"Humour me, Jack, please, just try, what harm will it do?"

His mother was right, as their village lay close to an airfield everyone was evacuating the village and moving to relatives further afield, including Martha.

Jack spent the next two days with Martha, visiting friends and relatives close by and enjoying each other's company for what could be the last time in a very long time. He spends their last moments memorising every feature of Martha's perfect face and wiping the tears from her rosy cheeks.

Jack looks her in the eyes and says, "I will be back, Martha, I promise, I will be back for you."

At that moment, he would have pinned his hopes on a dream or a wish on anything, give him a lamp to rub or a shooting star to wish upon. Martha takes the golden ribbon that is tying her hair up and hands it to Jack.

"Keep me with you always," she says before she gets into the car with her family and waves until she disappears into the distance.

He knew there were no guarantees though he couldn't tell her that he believed they were meant to be together and that not even this war would keep them apart.

The following morning, Jack receives a visit from his local army officer checking he has his orders and that he intends to comply. Of course, he does, if it weren't for an unfortunate accident, his father would have probably been joining him. Once the officer leaves, he starts to overthink the promise he has made to Martha. His mother and father decide to stay in the village until Jack is ready to head off to his barracks. On his way to walk the trails of the forest, Jack finds himself walking the streets of his emptying village and saying goodbye to people he has known all his life.

With his parents the last to leave the village, Jack has decided it is time to leave for basic training so that his parents can head to his aunt's. Having his morning cup of tea with his mother, he tells her of his plan. She is not happy about it, as he still has a few days they could spend together and that he could spend looking for the tree. Jack confesses that he has spent these last few days since Martha left wandering the woodland trails looking for such a tree. He tells her he plans to take a walk through the village and woodland trails one last time. On the way, he wants to post a letter for Martha through the letterbox at her family home. His bags are already packed for him to leave when he gets back, he hugs his mother tightly before setting off.

The village is eerily silent as he walks to Martha's, he takes the letter from his pocket, the ribbon she had given him from her hair came with it so he posts the letter and pockets the ribbon. Heading back to the village and on to the woods he played in as a child, he can't help thinking about the challenges to come. He thinks about the training his father had told him about, the intensity of the training to get you ready in hurry, the distance from home because he'd only been as far as the city to find a decent engagement ring for Martha and now he was going to be thrust into a situation, hundreds, if not thousands, of miles away. He hears the birds singing in the trees as he walks the trails, *will this be the last time I hear their song for a while.* My parents, what they went through, he doesn't want that for Martha, he wants nothing more than to return safely to his family and to his beloved fiancée.

Jack returns from his daydream and realises he is on an unfamiliar trail, he heads into a glen that is bathed in golden sunlight and as he walks further, sees the outline of a tree. Every time he blinks, its shadow is there behind his eyelids. As he draws closer to the tree, it is huge, the massive trunk is bigger than the floor space of the church back in the village. He looks up the tree to see that it has no leaves and no fruit, it's not autumn yet, thinks Jack. On closer inspection, he sees that the hundreds of branches above are covered in bows tied from countless types of material.

Why now? Having searched for the last few days how has he now come across the tree? He climbs the tree as high as he can and looks out across an unfamiliar valley. Jack starts to wonder where he is rather than how, he played in the forest near his home from a young age and this place is definitely not part of his local forest. He pulls the ribbon Martha gave him from his pocket and is torn, *do I tie the ribbon or keep it with me?*

As he sits at the base of the tree contemplating what is happening right now and what his wish or desire is. Making it back from war is the ultimate desire, if he manages to come back unscathed, then he can make it back to his family and his fiancée to finally marry the love of his life. The thought that if he ties Martha's ribbon to the tree it will not be with him while he is in strange lands haunts his thoughts. The dawning realisation is that he is in the presence of the ribbon tree his mother had told him about, as part of her miracle of having him. He climbs the tree again and ties the ribbon on an outreaching branch holding that desire to return from war and to those he loves.

Jack jumps down from the tree and lands in a bush, the bush wasn't there just a moment ago, as he looks around he is in the woodland he has known all his life. He rushes back home and into the living room where he finds his mother checking his bag, clearly making sure he has packed the essentials, as she looks up to see Jack's beaming smile he doesn't have to say a word, she knows.

Chapter 2
Eliza's Story

Eliza waits patiently at the station's edge, she hasn't heard from her Thomas in nearly three months and his unit is due home from the war in Europe. As she stares down the track, she has a joyful flashback to hearing the announcement on the wireless that at the eleventh hour on the eleventh day of the eleventh month the war had ended. She hadn't seen her Thomas in four years and his letters had been sparse, though they seemed to arrive just as she was beginning to worry for him. In the summer of 1914, he had gone from being a local grocery store clerk to frontline soldier as part of the allied response and now he is coming home, so that they can pick up the threads of their lives torn apart by war.

Several trains have been and gone, none were carrying returning soldiers, the station master steps out from his office to let the waiting families know that he is sure the next train arriving carries their loved ones. The train arrives and sure enough there they are, returning heroes exiting the carriages, some of the families were from Eliza's village and they kept checking back to see that she was still looking for her person. One of the soldiers, the Richardson's son, walks up to Eliza and tells her that Thomas did make it back from France and he was with them when they were rallying up for discharge though he hadn't seen him since.

"That was two days ago," he adds.

Eliza makes her way to the bus stop and is confused as to where he might be, she thought he would be home as soon as he could, especially as he hasn't written her in a while. As she walks up the path to the front door still lost in thought, she misses the young man sitting on the low retaining wall.

"Nice to see you too, my angel," the man calls out.

Eliza spins round to see Thomas standing with a crutch under one arm. As he looks at her, she has a look of disbelief.

"Don't worry, it's not as bad as it looks." He reassures her. When they get indoors and settle with a cup of tea, he explains that a couple of months ago, his unit came under fire and he had managed to get some shrapnel in his thigh which had seen him sent back to Blighty to patch him up and he has been through some surgery to get the movement back, though he admitted he had been on a lot of pain medication to do so.

She can't help but ask, "Why didn't you write me? I would have come to help you recover."

His answer is not what she was expecting.

"I didn't want to let you know in case I could never walk again, I thought you wouldn't want me."

She sets about straightening him out on a few things and making it perfectly clear they are one and nothing should come between them.

"So why weren't you on the train?" she asks.

"I missed it due to physiotherapy over running and so they arranged for a car to drop me off home instead."

As Thomas gets back to village life and recovers from his wounds, Eliza notices a difference in her husband, the kindness he always showed to everyone seemed to be lost, his temper was quick and sharp and he would swing from loving and thoughtful, to cruel and frightening in a snap.

Is this the effect war has had on the mild mannered grocery clerk she married?

Eliza never would have dreamed this could happen to her Thomas. As the months roll on, his mood swings increase in frequency and intensity and Eliza fears for their future and his state of mind.

On a walk through the village, Eliza bumps into Mrs Richardson, her son James returned on the train a few months ago and had given Eliza the news on Thomas, she was covering a black eye and bruised cheek.

"Oh my, whatever has happened!" Eliza exclaimed.

"Oh it's nothing, I went in to check on James, you see, as he was having some sort of nightmare. I just thought I'd get him to stop screaming."

In reality, James had sprung too when he was startled and began hitting his own mother uncontrollably until his father stepped in. Mrs Richardson explained that they had to call the doctor to check on James and the doctor had suggested this response was due to the war and how tightly wound up the men were, it was no excuse for his actions, the doctor had added and James was being seen by a specialist doctor in London.

Eliza finishes her walk having said hello to neighbours on her way to the forest to collect some firewood. On her return home, Thomas is sitting next to the fire nursing his thigh, looking up with an angry tone in his brow, he accuses Eliza of being gone so long she must be courting another suitor. She tells him he is being ridiculous and with that he attempts to launch himself at her with hand raised, stopping short of making contact with Eliza and realising what he is doing.

Eliza knows the only way she will get the man she loves back is if they have the family they always dreamed of. A child that will rekindle the love for life he always had. She bravely manages his temper and outbursts while attempting to engineer beautiful evenings for them to enjoy while trying to conceive a child. Months pass and Mrs Richardson updates Eliza that James has been taken to a psychiatric ward for help and support which has left Mr Richardson and herself in pieces, she asks how Thomas is doing and Eliza just lets her know that they are trying for a family, Mrs Richardson congratulates Eliza and wishes them the best.

A few months turn into a couple of years and Eliza is now losing hope, she has miscarried on so many occasions and is now scared that she might not be able to have children. This twist of fate is cruel, she thinks, though she is determined to keep her dream alive and her desire for the love of her life to return to her and for her to have, what she believes, is the perfect life, is unbreakable. In this time, young James, the Richardson's boy had been released from care only to come to a tragic end while riding a motorcycle. The Richardson's had decided to move away and start afresh in a new town or village shortly after James's funeral. Eliza suddenly recalls a strange conversation she had with Mrs Richardson at the wake for James.

"It was my fault, I wasn't clear with what I wanted, I just wanted James's nightmare to be over," Mrs Richardson had said.

At the time Eliza had just asked what she meant and Mrs Richardson had said the tree misunderstood her. Pondering that recollection for a moment, Eliza was in disbelief, there was an old wives' tale of a wishing tree but it was centuries old, was that what Mrs Richardson was referring to? Had she seen it?

Eliza walked the same woodland trails as Mrs Richardson did, she had never come across a strange tree that is said to bear no leaves or fruit and if the tales are true it is bathed in sunlight. Couldn't have been here, thinks Eliza, it's always overcast and raining. On her way for her daily walk, Eliza stops by Thomas at work, he is visibly in pain, she gives him a kiss and tells him everything will be as it should have been. She heads off to the woodland trails to collect firewood and also to see whether she can find a route that Mrs Richardson might have taken that could lead her to the mysterious wishing tree.

After weeks of walking different trails and at different times of day too, Eliza has found nothing. She sits on a fallen tree to rest for a moment and it dawns on her that she might be clutching at straws. She remembers how she and Thomas would walk these woods together when they were first in love and take picnics in the fields beyond and they both had agreed how perfect life would be, if they had a family once they were married and that their world would be complete. As Eliza stands to walk back to the village, the trail looks different, she has no memory of the shrubbery that is on the brow of a hill where she should be heading downhill, she is heading up. As she breaks through the shrubbery, there, bathed in golden sunlight, is the tree that bears no leaves or fruit. *This is a dream,* she thinks to herself, *I must have dozed off on the fallen tree,* she thinks this until she catches her hand on a thorn that shocks her. Now she has established this is not a dream, she knows what is it is she desires, and then the penny drops for her, until now she had desired finding the tree to help her and maybe the tree is only found when you know what it is you need help with the most and that didn't happen until she sat down for a rest and thought about Thomas and their beginnings and what they wanted for their future. When they met and fell in love there was no way of knowing whether Eliza could have a child. They were married and within no time whatsoever war broke out and took him from her, now with the tree's help, maybe she can get him back.

Eliza tears a strip of ribbon from her collar and climbs the tree, as she does she remembers what Mrs Richardson had said about being clear with her desire or wish. *What is it that I want,* she thinks. She wants her Thomas back from the despair he seems to be stuck in and for them to be the family they dreamed of, with a child that would make them whole. She ties the ribbon in a flowing bow as she holds that thought before climbing back down to the ground. *How do I get back?* She looks around and decides that the way she came in is as good as any, so heads back to the shrubs she came through. As she reaches the other side, she sees the fallen tree she had rested on and as she turns around, she sees the trail dropping back to the valley and the village in the distance, no shrubbery on the hill, no golden sunlight, just the way home.

Walking through the village, Eliza catches up to Thomas as he walks home, she holds his hand tightly and rolls around to hug him tightly.

With a smile on his face, he asks, "What's that for?"

She just replies, "I love you."

Nine months have passed by since the visit to the tree and Eliza sits huffing and puffing in bed as the midwife and doctor tell her to control her breathing. The baby is nearly here; Thomas paces the hallway outside waiting to hear the latest or the hint of a scream of one other than his wife.

"That's the baby crowned, Eliza, a few more big pushes and you'll meet your child," says the midwife.

She continues to breathe through the pain and calls for Thomas to be by her side which the midwife obliges and Thomas walks into a scene he couldn't comprehend from the other side of the door where he thought he would be better off in case his war trauma resurfaces at the sight of blood and screaming.

Instead, he moves straight to Eliza's side and holds her hand, commending her bravery and how amazing she is not just now, always. The final push and the baby comes clear, the midwife cleans and prepares him for the doctor to examine, the baby has a good set of lungs, the all clear is given and the midwife turns and says, "Are you ready to meet your son?"

Eliza looks at Thomas who has tears running down his face.

"Jack," she says, "Let's meet our son, Jack."

Just then, Eliza sees him, the man she knew was there, had found his way back and her heart was full as Thomas cradled both Jack and herself. She closed her eyes when the doctor's light caught her and there, behind closed lids, she saw it, the ribbon tree.

Chapter 3
Evelyn's Story

For one teenager, 1966 is an awful year, she has no interest in the world cup that is heading to the country in the next few months she is fixed on getting good grades in her science exams. Evelyn wants nothing more than to become a doctor, she wants to spearhead research into fertility and has a passion for genetics which, as she is told far too often, is strange for a girl her age.

What she really hears when her teachers tell her, "That's no job for a woman", her determination is unparalleled she knows that more and more couples are struggling to become families and she wants to help fix this.

Evelyn's desire to help those couples comes from the stories her grandmother, Granny E, used to tell her about women who couldn't have children feeling broken. From a young age her grandmother would tell her that she had been unable to have children herself. Growing up with this pain in her own family she always wanted to do something to help and her caring nature pushed her to achieve her goals. In the current climate, there are social inequalities that she is having to deal with, her determination will not be swayed though.

A graduate position awaits once these exams are done, with the hopes of being a doctor, Evelyn will join a team that are looking into the chromosomes that could cause issues when looking to conceive. As it is early days, in their study they are keen to be seen as a forward thinking outfit and want to be seen to be for women. Evelyn is a little proud though not enough to let this fact get in her way. Her family have always been there for their country, her grandfather fought in the first world war and only decades later, her father was involved in the second world war. She sees this as her own personal war that she has to win.

The summer comes and goes, as it happens England won the world cup, not that that mattered to Evelyn having just turned 20, she can't wait to find out what the future holds. Exam results are being posted soon and that day can't come soon enough.

Evelyn's father keeps telling her, "We're proud of you, no matter the outcome."

She replies each time with, "Thanks for the support, it will all be for nothing though if I can't make a difference."

Her father and mother have an amazing love story that she and her siblings would be told over and over as children. Some of the details escape her she just remembers he made it back from the second world war unscathed to return and marry her mother. That eternal optimism is her dream, she wants to make a difference and have an amazing life where she can make her Granny E proud a lot. She knows it's what she wants more than ever.

That fateful day arrives and her results are posted at the school for her to check. Evelyn struggles for the first time, she is feeling really anxious. Her mother steps up to the boards and searches for her results.

"Evelyn, you need to see this," her mother calls, as she looks to where her mother is pointing there they are a mixture of A's and B's and more than what she needed to take up the post with the new research team.

She hugs her mother and breathes a sigh of relief, she knows the hard work starts now.

A balding man with a smile and glasses approaches as Evelyn walks into the genetics' team building for the first time.

"Welcome, Evelyn, I'm Dr Stevens, we've spoken on the telephone a few times and it is nice to finally meet you."

As time would have it that was the first and only nice greeting she would hear from his lips. Evelyn knew this was a public relation's role to show women involved in the development of fertility treatment, her hope is that she can have a positive impression on the research and maybe influence its development. From that first day, she has found herself passing the laboratories where the work is going on and, like the other women in the team, they find themselves fetching tea and typing up notes. The four of them are then put out front with Dr Stevens whenever the press or board members have questions.

As a group they have had enough and Evelyn organises a meeting with the other women in the team and they compare notes from what they have read and as they thought the research team are getting nowhere with a breakthrough. They meet up every week to discuss the research while preparing teas and coffees and work out the steps that are missing. They see that they are not concentrating on the process of encouraging more egg production, they are not even in the right area of thinking. When the women start to question the notes they are typing up, Dr Stevens and his team take their comments and interjection as an insult. Evelyn and the others explain that they are qualified to help and want to be part of the solution not the problem and the problem is clear, this team has no idea where to start. Another media briefing for the scientific journals and Evelyn is wheeled out to support one of Dr Steven's team, a Dr Andrews, she hasn't been in the press room with him before though the others say he is not very confident.

"So how is the development of the treatment going?" Comes a question from the crowd, without thinking, "Not very well at the moment!" Evelyn exclaims.

A clearly shaken Dr Andrews stares at her in disbelief.

"How so?" The response comes from the audiences.

It is this opportunity Evelyn has been waiting for, she grabs it with both hands.

"The focus thus far has been on what is not working and that is clear. There is a link between low egg counts and infertility and all the research so far has been confirming this." Evelyn explains.

"So how do you propose moving forward?" A question comes from a member of the board.

"We need to concentrate efforts on a formula that can help increase the production of eggs in those women who are unable to conceive." She continues by explaining this will be something that takes time and may need to be small doses over time and that they are yet to experiment with this potential line of treatment.

At the rear of the auditorium stands Dr Stevens with a very unimpressed look on his face.

"You were supposed to sit there and nod and agree. That is your role here, Evelyn, what the hell have you just done!"

Her response is calm and measured. "My job, Dr Stevens, I came here to help those women unable to conceive, not to deceive the board or the public with this nonsense that you have us typing up and sending out to the scientific community."

"You are off this team, Evelyn, do you hear me!" His tone is clear and with no support from anyone else in the room, she feels that impending sense of failure, she can't believe this is happening.

Evelyn leaves the office, there are a few days until the weekend and she plans to see her Granny E. She feels it only right to let her know what has happened and how she has let her down. At that moment, she remembers the stories from her parents, she remembers them talking about an old tree and something about ribbons and how it had saved Granny E and her grandfather after he was damaged by the first world war and also how her father had visited it and his wish came true, is it a wishing tree? Is it to do with desires? Evelyn can't sleep and she doesn't want to ask Granny E about some tree that might have been a bedtime story. She visits her local library and begins pulling books on the oldest known trees as well as fables and history. There has to be mention of where it is, *can she find it and discuss it with Granny E,* she thinks, also it should be easy to find. Her parents and Granny E still live in the same village and both found it in the same woodland, albeit from different locations. While she knows this is silly, she feels it will keep her mind occupied for a couple of days until she heads back home to break the news about her career.

As she scans through a book of mystical events during Egyptian times, she sees something. Initially, she thought it was a palm tree in the hieroglyphics and on double taking she sees a tree different to others. She has no idea about hieroglyphs and scans the page to see what is written and there is something about the first pharaohs creating their empire with the help of a tree of desire and that if your desire is worthy, it will be made so. The early pharaohs wanted to have a civilisation that would shape the future and that is what the world got. *I can't believe it,* she thinks; *could this be the same tree?* If so Granny E has never left the country so how did she get to Egypt? More questions arrive as she looks into the South American tribes and Incas only to come across a hieroglyph resembling the same tree. The story tells in the book of a great tree of offering that gave plentiful harvests and one day it was not to be found and for its return they would sacrifice villagers only for the sun to arrive and kill the crops and the land and so sacrifices would be made to appease the sun. She searches and searches seeing it appear in Norse mythology referred to as the great tree of life and in other times and countries other civilisations and cultures though nothing in recent years, until, a newspaper article from a local London paper about a woman who moved to the borough recently and went mad from the loss of her son who she blamed on herself and the wishing tree! As she reads on, the woman, a Mrs Richardson, was originally from the village she grew up in and where her family still lives. Granny E would surely know her.

As the weekend arrives, Evelyn makes her way home to her family, she calls in to see her mother and father and tell them what transpired in the recent briefing. After dropping her bags, she makes her way over to see Granny E, there she finds Granny E tending her roses and with a click of the gate swinging to her feet and turning with a big smile.

"My little, Evelyn, how are you, my darling girl?"

She can see the look of disappointment in her granddaughter's eyes and without further ado suggests they take a walk to the town which was just through the forest.

"Let's have lunch in town, there is a new cafe that is supposed to be wonderful, my treat."

Granny E puts down her pruning shears and they head back out the gate and past her parents' house, a glancing wave to let them know they were okay. While walking through the woods, there is nothing but silence, neither one wants to speak.

Granny E breaks first. "What is it, my dear, are you alright?" she asks.

"No, Granny E, I am not."

She goes on to tell her about the ordeal she has been through and that it has been nearly two years since she started at the laboratory with no progress and being treated like a tea-maid until that is, when she did what she did, at the media update, she even recalled the board member addressing her directly. Suddenly, it seemed worse.

They arrive at the cafe and take a seat next to one another, they order when the owner drops by and makes small talk with them. Evelyn asks about Mrs Richardson and whether Granny E was aware of her passing.

"No, my dear, I had no idea, Mrs Richardson and her husband moved away to London shortly after their son died in an awful motorcycle accident."

Evelyn asks, "Is that what she meant by it was her fault and the tree didn't understand what she meant?"

Granny E was curious to know how she had come to know this and Evelyn explained that before her own passing Mrs Richardson had been in a local newspaper back in London and had made these exclamations in public. Granny E does her best to retell what happened with Mrs Richardson's son and that her own grandfather had returned in much the same way, a broken man. As they enjoy the afternoon and some fantastic food, Evelyn can't help but wonder what difference could she have made, why wasn't she given the chance to make that difference. Granny E settles up the bill and they head back home through the forest. A slight chill in the air on the way back, sees Granny E take off her embroidered scarf and place it around Evelyn's neck.

As they walk through the forest they reminisce about when Evelyn, along with her brother and sister, would play for hours in the trees of the forest. Just then, Evelyn snagged her Granny E's scarf on a thorn and as she turns to release the scarf, the wind has died down and there is glorious sunshine upon a golden meadow and there on a hill is the outline of a tree she is now so aware of, she has seen it in hieroglyph, she has seen it in photos of old scrolls and it fits the description of each account. As she reaches the ribbon tree, she realises she doesn't have any ribbon and what is it that she desires? What will she wish for? From what she's read, she has an idea of how this works and as long as she is certain of what she wants, will it make a difference? She knows one thing that she has always wanted and tries to stay focused on that, still there is the fact she is missing a piece of ribbon. So why has the tree appeared if she is helpless to ask for its help? As she sits at the base of the tree looking up, it seems there is an endless number of branches and she thinks about all the wishes and desires, the hopes, the dreams, the reality that some of them will have been tied so long ago that none of this makes sense.

Evelyn begins to wonder whether Granny E is searching for her and how worried she might be, as she sits and continues to look up at the tree in all its glory, she becomes aware she is twiddling Granny E's scarf. The snag on the bush has pulled the stitching and the ribbon edge has become exposed, Evelyn is so pleased that this opportunity has come to her and she knows it will not be wasted if she gets to make a difference. Taking a firm grip on the lower branches she starts the climb, she feels as though she is being drawn to a branch and keeps moving. Settling herself on a bow that feels right she shuffles along to a clearing, as she frees a piece of ribbon from the scarf she notices a similar piece tied nearby, it's almost identical. Ribbon ready, she gathers her thoughts and takes time to think about why she is here and why the tree has appeared for her, this is an opportunity that may never come again, yet she is the third generation of her family that the tree has appeared for even then is that right, had it appeared before then.

"Getting off track, Evelyn," she says out loud, refocused and with that desire to make a difference in her field of fertility treatment and give that glimmer of hope to couples that struggle to conceive.

The ribbon is tied, she placed it next to the identical ribbon and as she climbs down, it fades into her distant view, indistinguishable from the others on the branches. She reaches the bottom and turning from the tree she is back in the forest. Granny E just ahead of her and the scarf snagged on a thorn. She unhooks the scarf, noticing a piece of the ribbon missing and turns to Granny E, *was it a day dream? Did she get it right?*

So many questions that will remain unanswered and only time will tell if it actually happened and if so, will she get what she desires?

"I'm so sorry, Granny E, I will get you another one, where did you get it from?"

"Your father made it for me when he started his tailoring business after the war, that's his favourite ribbon."

Granny E sees the tears forming in Evelyn's eyes and says with all reassurance, "It's all going to be okay, my darling."

Chapter 4
Thomas's Story

Sitting at his desk, Thomas can see the city skyline and the birds flying high in the distance. As he concentrates, he hears the sounds of the bustling streets below. Daydreaming has become the norm for him, for near twenty years he has been trying to write a book about a subject that publishers will not accept as a work of non-fiction.

Thomas is fortunate, he is the son of a famous doctor and the grandson of a celebrated Saville row tailor. The unfortunate thing is that he lives off their success and has done so since leaving university and now more than ever he is feeling the weight of disappointment, his younger brother is a geneticist who works at a celebrated teaching hospital in Switzerland and his baby sister is a famous sports personality. As the older sibling, he finds it hard to understand why both of them still look up to him, after all they did grow up with the same stories he did when it came to his family.

It all began when his great grandmother, Eliza, went in search of a mysterious tree. Her desire was to restore the love of her husband, Thomas who is also the great grandfather he is named after. His great grandfather returned from war a changed man due to injury and the horrors he saw yet on one fateful day, Eliza, full of hope, set off in search of the tree of wishes or desires, this is the element he is still unsure on. As it happens, the belief is that the tree found her and tying a ribbon to a branch of this tree she wanted her husband back from this despair and then a miracle happened, Eliza was unable to bear children, or so they thought because she fell pregnant shortly after the visit with the tree and on his grandfather's birth a bright light with the shadow of the tree burnt into it was behind Eliza's eyelids.

He fast forwards and his grandfather, Jack, looks for or is visited by the tree as he wants nothing more than to return safely to Thomas's grandmother, Martha. Jack would tell Thomas stories of the war and how the tree seemed to be watching over him, in any action he was involved in, the burning light with the shadow of the tree would blind him in time to miss a mortar strike or stop him stepping on a landmine and he never saw it again after returning from war. He married the love of his life and one of his children Evelyn became a renowned scientist that was instrumental in the creation of IVF treatment for women that struggled to have a baby. Now he is really intrigued with this story as it is his mother's, she researched the tree and its origins and was unable to get to the bottom of what it was or where it came from and after her time with it, she looked no further. She would tell him that she lost her job as a front person for a scientific group looking into fertility treatment and at one briefing she spoke out of turn, she was let go and after the visit to the tree it turned out one of the board of directors was at the briefing and had asked a question and her response impressed them so much they met her when she went to clear her draw out and asked her to head up the research and there it was, his mother's bright light and shadow of the tree moment.

"What a loser." He thinks to himself, surrounded by success and here he still sits, his family have been supporting his research and life since university.

This is their story more than his and he wants to be the one that explains the mystery behind the tree, he has spent the better years of his life frustrating his friends around him as they disappear from his table after marriage, they move away then start families and he is nowhere near that point in his life so has lost touch with so many of them. The days are blurring into one another and visiting museums and libraries has become repetitive and he still has so much to cover, there has to be a link, a start, and after all it can't be coincidence that generations of his family have been in its presence and yet no one is any the wiser as to what it is and why it exists, what is its purpose? What is worse is no one seems to want to follow it up though they have all been generous with their time and money to help him with his investigation.

Thomas's ever dwindling circle of friends is about to shrink further, every declaration of love turns into a marriage proposal, with every wedding and with every child conceived, they seem to move away. A recent catch up with Dion has resulted in his last college and university friend asking him to be best man at his very own wedding.

"You gotta be kidding me, Dion, you sure this is the right move?" Speaking without thinking, Thomas realises the error in his words. "I'm sorry, mate, thank you for asking me, it would be my honour."

They spend the rest of their time discussing when and where this event will take place. Before they finish their last drink, Dion is concerned about Thomas, he knows that soon Thomas will be the only one from their circle that has no one and has seen all their friends move away once they have kids to be in the towns surrounding the city where it is more affordable for them and clearly sees the same in his future.

"So what will you do my friend?" he asks in a concerned tone. "Is there anyone on the horizon for you?"

Thomas shakes his head and confesses that not only is he alone, he is still unable to find the mythical tree's location and so he is neither lucky in love or his work.

The following day, he wakes and realises finally that there is no tree for him, this was to be his crowning moment and the crown has most definitely been made of thorns and is weighing heavy at the moment. A quick call to Dion to see whether his company is hiring, moves Thomas toward the employment ladder, time to stand on his own two feet instead of the kindness of his family is the new mind-set and it is time to face reality. With this change in focus so late in life, Thomas can't help but think about the opportunities that presented themselves in life and love from university to research work in South America. His mind wanders to Sophia, his university girlfriend, her patience ran out a few years after they graduated when his focus was purely on proving the existence of a mystical or mythical tree that seems to grant wishes or fulfil your greatest desire, this is still unknown and the element that continued to fuel the passion to answer the questions. The passion was misplaced and Sophia could not compete with the obsession he had and still has.

As luck would have it, Dion's company is hiring, they are a market research company that Dion has explained on numerous occasions and Thomas has never understood what they do. With a good word put in for him he is apprehensive to say the least, Thomas has never done a 9 to 5 job and has no idea what he's going to say when they ask him career questions to check his suitability to any job, let alone one with a title as confusing as the assistant research analyst to the managing director which sounds like a great deal of responsibility. A wave of fear washes over Thomas as he tries to create a credible appearance with prepared questions and as many responses to the inevitable barrage of queries as to why take a job now?

Dion is all smiles as Thomas walks into the lobby of his office building and embraces him, such a welcome was not expected and it would appear that Dion has already spoken to those conducting the interview so now there is more pressure not to mess it up.

"I'll meet you in the lobby when you're done, Tom, okay?"

"Sure thing, Dion, wish me luck."

"You've got this, mate, honestly, lunch is on me, I'll see you in a bit", and just like that a new career and a new horizon presents itself and that feeling of failure and dread drains Thomas.

Waiting to be called through for his interview, Thomas is taking stock of all he's learnt about this mystical tree and how little he still knows about its origin or location and if it was his wish to learn more about the tree why hasn't it appeared or called him to it? Could it be as simple as because he wants nothing more than to get answers about the tree that is then the reason it alludes him? A host of new thoughts about this now of all times when suddenly he snaps out of a daydream to the sound of his name being called.

"Hi, Thomas, I am Dan Simmons, Dion has told us so much about you, please, come through."

Two weeks later, and having impressed Mr Simmons, Thomas finds himself sitting at a desk with little to do but daydream and now being paid for it in contrast to sitting at his desk at home and getting support from family. There are still those thoughts that are newly formed and giving him sleepless nights and day time dreaming sessions, how does the tree decide? What do you have to do or want for it to deem you worthy of its presence or indeed for you to be given an audience? As he is now in gainful employ Thomas decides it is time to visit his family and let them know what has transpired and to apologise for not answering the family question about the tree. This is likely to be an uncomfortable visit as the question will still stand, why now? There is definitely an element of the conversations with Dion prior to this change in direction though now their catch ups are about stag do plans and wedding attire. A break from the city might just be what he needs after all it has been months since he last visited the family and this life change should be delivered and definitely discussed in person.

The train journey reminds Thomas of his namesake who was supposed to have made this journey when he returned from the first world war, his great grandmother was meant to meet him and he wasn't aboard. With a judder, the train pulls into the station and the doors open onto the platform, there with a wide smile and arms wider still, is his mother, Evelyn.

"Thought I'd pick you up instead of grabbing a taxi," she says while wrapping him tightly in her embrace.

Would she still be so welcoming when he says what he has come to say? It's too early in the visit to drop into conversation that he has completely changed how he is living his life and his direction. On the journey back, they talk instead about Dion's planned wedding and being best man, his mother offers to send him some money so that he can pay for a decent stag do, or at least the deposit, she notices his face drop and can't help but ask, "What is wrong, Thomas? Are you okay? How is your research coming? Any answers yet?"

His response is curt and out of character. "I'm done with the research, there is nothing to support what it is or where it originates, so I got a job, okay?"

The rest of the journey was spent in an awkward silence, as they pulled up the driveway to his family home, Thomas apologises for his outburst.

"I've been searching for what seems like forever, Mum, there is reference to the tree throughout time just as you found when you searched and that is just it, there is no further detail, even you are unable to give me anything more to go on."

"There's nothing more to tell, darling, honest, I've told you my experience and told you about your great granny E's experience and you've spoken to Grandad. I don't know what else we can offer; does this mean you're dropping the dream you've been chasing all these years?"

He doesn't respond, just stares wildly into the distance clearly controlling tears, that are desperate to escape. They head indoors after getting Thomas's bag from the boot of the car. Thomas's mother lets him know that his nan and grandad will be over for dinner later and a better chat can take place when they are all together. She seems desperate for answers and agitated by how whimsically he has thrown away everything he has worked for since university.

Thomas heads to his old room and puts his bag down, sitting on the corner of his bed a glance to the bookshelf by the window seeing it is still full of his notebooks and history books from his teens. He pulls one of the notebooks and scans what he had written, when his obsession started. He noted every time his family had told him their story he wrote the date and time and the very words they said. As he reads their story, he notices that never once does the wording change, every time he was told the story by his great grandmother he looks for a variation in the wording, no the wording is the same on every occasion. He checks the notebook for his grandfather and it is the same different dates and different times of day the words used are the same, he knows the answer and checks anyway, his mother's are identical too. He remembers that he used to record them and play it back so he could write it down and the tapes he used must be in the loft because he always kept hold of everything due to his fascination with the tree. As a teenager, he clearly hadn't seen this pattern and now he can see it clear as day, so the only question to answer is … what does it mean?

As his grandparents arrive for dinner, Thomas still has the question burning in his mind, walking down the stairs he hears his grandparents talking to his mother though he is unable to make out what is being said.

During dinner their conversation becomes clear. "So your mother tells us you've got a regular job."

"That's right, Pops," replies Thomas.

"What happened with your research into the ribbon tree?" asks his grandmother.

"I have been going around and around in circles for years Marmar, I have been wasting your time, my life and your money looking into something that doesn't seem to have a known origin or even an early educated guess as to what it is or where it's from"

"Your passion for the stories of the tree is why we thought you'd be able to unravel the mystery behind it, Thomas," adds Grandpa Jack.

Thomas has his notebooks with him and suggests that after dinner he has some one-to-one time with Grandpa Jack and his mum. He intends to get them to retell their experience so he can check what is said against what was written years ago as surely with time passing the story would have changed or deviated in some way after all it has been probably a decade since they last regaled their tale.

They finish desert and Thomas takes his wine and Grandpa Jack to the study.

"What's this about, lad?" asks Grandpa Jack.

"I just want you to tell me your story of the tree again, just in case I missed something."

With notebook open at the last entry for Grandpa Jack, he begins to tell his story of wanting nothing more than to be able to return to his beloved Martha and as he continues to tell the tale, the words used are exactly the same, no actual details about the tree just the desire and the tying of the ribbon on a branch.

As Grandpa Jack finishes his tale, Thomas asks what he remembers of the tree itself and its surroundings, Grandpa Jack says, "Well, I've just told you, haven't I?"

"No, Grandpa, you tell me a lovely tale of surviving world war II and making it back to Marmar and that you visited the tree, the information missing is what type of tree? What surroundings are there?"

Jack looks confused, he would swear blind he had described the tree and when asked again about the variety of tree he draws a blank. Thomas then follows the same pattern with his mother and faces the same outcome exactly the same words used to describe her visit to the tree, he continues to think why these members of his family? Why did it choose his great granny E, why Grandpa Jack or his mother? There stories offer no more of an insight into the tree, the interest is now in the individuals though again what is the connection?

The weekend draws to an end, Thomas's family reluctantly accept the fact he has decided to completely upheave his life and move in a different direction. All packed in the car, his mother decides they should stop for lunch in town before he catches his train, having grabbed a space outside the cafe they take a seat and look over the menu. For his mother this is a special place because she used to visit this cafe with her granny E before she passed away and it was here that she had lunch before the tree appeared to her. The waitress arrives to take their order and as Thomas looks up, he sees a familiar face.

"Sophia!" he exclaims.

"Wow, hi, Thomas, long time no see, how are you doing?" she says with a smile.

"Not bad, as it happens, I have taken a break from my research and book and have a job with Dion's company, how are you?"

"Congratulations! I hope Dion is well, we've just had the invite to his wedding. It's been ages. After London, I met my husband and we moved down here for a business opportunity that came up and we've been here going on five years now and with plans to open another cafe later in the year."

"That's fantastic, I am sorry this is my mother," he says with a subdued tone.

"No I remember your mother, Thomas."

They enjoy their lunch, with Thomas thinking about whether that is how his life with Sophia would have turned out, marriage and a business enterprise maybe even kids.

The train ride home had Thomas more conflicted than ever, having gained some support from his family for his change of heart he can't help wondering who the change is for, his life to date has been trying to document the location and meaning of this elusive tree that has had such a profound influence on his family and now he knows that there seems to be something missing from those that have been in the tree's presence … They are unable to recall the tree itself they can't recall the species of tree it looks like (given it has no leaves or fruit) or how tall it is which is new information for him to work with. When he adds to this meeting Sofia after so long and hearing how her life has turned out, it dawns on Thomas that he has never really known what he wants out of life and yet he has lived the majority of it in solitude and now has decided to change direction because of his guilt that he has been living off his family and his fear of being alone has seen him move into a mainstream job. Is this coincidence, fate or a plan? A plan to stop him looking into the origins of the tree and like a splash of cold water to the face, he stops dead in his thoughts as this rabbit hole is ridiculous and one where he is putting his failings and fears on a tree he has never seen and in his own mind fabricating that it, the tree, is influencing these decisions. With an hour left of his journey he changes the album he is listening to on his phone and closes his eyes.

Mondays are the worst for Thomas, for so many years he was used to a leisurely start to the day, which he now appreciates to be lazy laying in, that alarm at 0600 hrs to get ready and head to an office desk and daydream pretty much all day with little work to do in-between. Dion had messaged to say he wasn't in today due to coming back from a venue visit for the wedding so even lunch was going to be a solitary thing today. With the weekend's events still fresh in Thomas's mind, he starts to daydream about everything that he said and saw this weekend from his old notebooks to Sophia. Before he knows it, his head is resting on his folded arms rested on his desk.

A bright light makes Thomas sit bolt upright in his chair, has he just been caught taking a nap at his desk?

Great, I'm going to get fired and I've only just told the family about my job, he thinks to himself.

As he regains focus, he thinks he must be dreaming, he is not sitting at his desk, though he is sitting on a rock in an outcropping and his head was clearly resting against the rock next to him, this is apparent by the drool spot. As he looks around it must be a dream, for around the rock is a golden meadow and on a hill in the distance a shape he is only too familiar with. Reality quickly catches up with him, as he slips off the rock and rolls his ankle, the shooting pain would have woken him if he were asleep and the fact it stings like hell must mean he is awake.

As Thomas moves through the meadow, he sees large stones similar to those at Stonehenge and they have markings on them which he moves closer to see, as he can't quite make them out. On closer inspection there are carvings from different civilisations, he recognises Mesopotamian, he can see Mayan and Egyptian, there are Runic carvings and on checking his pockets he doesn't have his camera phone in his pocket to record this. He can't help but think why now? Why after all this time has the tree appeared? He spends time looking around the meadow and seeing rocks and stones of different shapes and sizes with markings from all eras and some he has absolutely no idea where they came from. What is his desire? What is the wish or fate that has brought him here? So many questions and no one to answer them. He feels as though he has been in the meadow for hours trying to decipher dead languages with some referring to it as a tree of destiny while other hieroglyphs refer to it as a wishing tree or tree of desire, the runic refers to it though as Yggdrasil which is the tree that binds the realms in Norse mythology. Making his way to the tree, Thomas wonders how much of this he will remember and all those people throughout his life that have doubted its existence, what will they think? The tree gets ever closer and while he is not the best at dendrology he is unsure of the tree's species himself. With his hand on the trunk of the great tree he walks to its mighty base all the while looking up to see the tree disappear into the vantage point of his vision.

"So why have you brought me here now of all times?" Thomas asks the tree, almost expecting a reply. "You clearly don't let those you visit or that visit you recall much of the encounter and you should know by now, meeting you has been all I've wanted for so long."

Still no reply from the tree, feeling a bit foolish, he sits at the base of the tree and rests his head back against the trunk and as his head touches the trunk, he feels a sensation and closes his eyes and in an instant he imagines that the tree had met his great grandmother as she had to give birth to his grandfather for if Jack was not born he could not visit the tree to fulfil his destiny to return home to Thomas's Marmar and in turn it shows him that they arrive at the tree's ultimate visitor… Evelyn, Thomas's mother, as without his grandfather she would not exist and her pioneering spirit and work toward IVF and fertility would mean there would be fewer souls to touch as no one else would have the desire to solve the issue of fertility like she would all because she was so passionate to solve it in honour of her own Granny E.

"If that was you showing me that and not me just putting two and two together, that is unbelievable."

Thomas is still unable to work out why the tree has visited him or given him an audience and with so many emotions and thoughts running through his head, he feels the best thing to do is find his spot on the tree and tie the nearest thing he has to ribbon, some of the lining from his trouser pocket, to a branch and trust what the tree has in store for him.

As he climbs and clings to a limb, he finds a space on a branch and pulls the lining from his trouser pocket, he tears a ribbon strip from it and places the rest in his good pocket. Trusting the tree, he ties his ribbon and lets out a deep breath he had been holding. That's it, the bond is made and he descends slowly, observing the long limbs and many branches of the tree with all the colourful bows clear to see and some shimmering in the golden glow.

He jumps down from the lowest branch and with a slight ache in his ankle, he sits up, he is at his desk at work, he stands though his ankle is still sore and he can feel his mobile phone sliding down the inside of his trouser leg. Thomas feels inside the pocket and the lining is missing, some of the remnants are in his other pocket, he retrieves his mobile from the floor and remembers, not the tree species or detail of the location instead he can remember why the members of his family had visited or been visited by the tree. Even with a sore ankle, he jumps around like a man possessed and drops into his boss's office to let him know that he will be tendering his resignation.

Three years have passed since the visit of the tree and Thomas is putting the finishing touches to his outfit, he had to agree to it being a work of fiction but he managed to write a worldwide bestselling book that became a Hollywood movie with a spinoff TV series all based on the tree of desires and wishes. Tonight, Thomas is attending a special meet and greet dinner gala to celebrate the book, its success worldwide and meet some of the fans of his work.

On the ride over to the venue, Thomas recalls the day he finished the book and thought he was about to get his bright light and shadow of the tree moment and even as his publisher announced the books first run had sold out, it still didn't happen.

His mother is beside him in the car, turns to him and with tears in her eyes she says to him, "You make us all so proud Thomas, you have no idea what all you have done means to me, Grandpa Jack and Granny E will be looking down on you, we all love you and you deserve this, my darling, you really do."

"Thank you, Mum, for all your support, I definitely couldn't have done it without you." As he finishes, the car door opens and they are escorted into the building.

Through the doors, Thomas can hear the master of ceremony introducing him and the doors open with a standing ovation, he begins moving through the tables and past family, friends and fans alike. As he gets toward the stage, he notices a woman clutching tight a copy of his book, must be a first run and well-read by the state of the cover, he makes his way over to her and asks her name.

"Nora," the pretty fan replies before adding, "would it be too much to get your autograph, you have no idea just how much of a lifesaver your book has been for me."

Thomas smiles and says, "Sure, do you have a pen?"

As she passes him the book and a pen, their hands touch and there it is, the bright light and shadow of the tree.

"Did you see it too?" asks Nora.

"Did I see what?" replies Thomas.

"The ribbon tree."

Chapter 5
Nora's Story

The letterbox clatters at Nora's front door, she retrieves what looks like a postcard from the drop box. Postcard it is not, she can't contain her excitement, no it must be a hoax, she thinks and immediately calls her friends to find out who is behind this elaborate prank. After speaking to all her friends, it appears she is definitely holding an invite to a gala being held tonight in town for her favourite author. This author's book gave her hope that there were others out there that had been seen by a mysterious tree. Nora herself has stood in the presence of the ribbon tree and she knew exactly why she was there. Nora had been very unlucky in love and had a string of not very nice partners who treated her badly for no other reason than they thought they could and at her lowest, just when she was about to give up on love the tree appeared.

A quick call to work to say, "I will be too ill to come in today", gave Nora a chance to go shopping for the right dress for this occasion and also she wanted to take her copy of *'The Tree of Destiny'* with her, even if it is very rough around the edges.

Having shopped all day and finding the perfect dress or three, Nora returned home to be greeted by her friend and flatmate Lottie. Lottie could not believe Nora's luck, living with her she has heard about the book, read the book and still is none the wiser as to why Nora finds it so special. For Nora this is because she has never told anyone about her visit to the ribbon tree. Lottie helps her to finish her hair and makeup before she gets a taxi into town.

Arriving at the grand old building, she is early, she thought it best, in case it turned out to be a prank and she would then be able to disappear before too many people were in the admission line. No not a prank she thinks as the security team take her pass and guide her to the seating plan, she finds her table, as it happens it is very close to the stage. Clutching her first run copy of his book she heads to the table placing the book on the surfacing and having a drink for Dutch courage.

The master of ceremony takes to the stage and introduces the author, everyone stands and claps his entrance and even in her heels Nora is struggling to see him. Turning back to the table, Nora picks up her copy of the book and as she turns, there he is in her line of sight and what's more he is heading in this direction.

The author asks her name.

"Nora," she replies and then cheekily adds, "would it be too much to get your autograph, you have no idea just how much of a lifesaver your book has been for me."

The author smiles at her and says, "Sure, do you have a pen?"

As she takes a pen from her purse, she passes it to him along with the book and as his hand touches hers she sees a bright light with the shadow of the ribbon tree, in her head she is thinking, *is this him, is he the one, I wanted nothing more than to find my true love, it surely can't be him* and as she looks at his face he seems to be recovering too, so she asks, "Did you see it too?"

"Did I see what?" he replies.

"The ribbon tree."

Chapter 6
Thomas & Nora's Story

Five years on from a chance meeting at a gala to celebrate his book, Thomas and Nora find themselves in a coffee shop of a bustling town, their intention the same as always, to visit bookstores and libraries wherever they go and move Thomas's book from the fiction to non-fiction aisle. Their guerrilla tactics born from their love for one another and the fact that both of them are fully aware the tree exists, after all the tree gave to Thomas and Nora exactly what they desired most.